For Estith—I'm glad we both left home to find each other
For Rafael and Alejandro—our greatest adventures
—L. B.

To Pilar and Jeanne,
for the nearly polar winters they've
spent together
—C. V.

STERLING CHILDREN'S BOOKS
New York

An Imprint of Sterling Publishing Co., Inc.
1166 Avenue of the Americas
New York, NY 10036

Text © 2018 Lindsay Bonilla
Cover and interior illustrations © 2018 Cinta Villalobos

ISBN 978-1-4549-2870-6

Distributed in Canada by Sterling Publishing Co., Inc.
c/o Canadian Manda Group, 664 Annette Street
Toronto, Ontario M6S 2C8, Canada
Distributed in the United Kingdom by GMC Distribution Services
Castle Place, 166 High Street, Lewes, East Sussex BN7 1XU, England
Distributed in Australia by NewSouth Books
45 Beach Street, Coogee, NSW 2034, Australia

For information about custom editions, special sales, and premium and corporate purchases,
please contact Sterling Special Sales at 800-805-5489 or specialsales@sterlingpublishing.com.

Manufactured in China

Lot #:
2 4 6 8 10 9 7 5 3 1
07/18

sterlingpublishing.com

Cover and interior design by Jo Obarowski
The artwork in this book was created digitally.

POLAR BEAR ISLAND

by **LINDSAY BONILLA**   illustrated by **CINTA VILLALOBOS**

STERLING CHILDREN'S BOOKS
New York

POLAR BEAR ISLAND was peaceful and predictable.
Parker, the mayor, planned to keep it that way.

But Kirby waddled where the wind blew, and today she was floating toward paradise.

"Didn't you read the sign?" asked Parker. "Get out!"

"I've had a long journey," said Kirby. "Please let me stay for the night."

"One night. No more!" Parker stomped away.

Kirby opened her suitcase.
Some curious polar bears peeked out of their dens.
"What are you doing?" they asked.

"I'm looking for my Flipper Slippers," said Kirby. "They keep your flippers and feet warm. Plus they're reversible! With one side you can skate on ice. With the other you can wade through snow."

"*Ooh!*" said the bears. "Do they work on paws?"

"I want a pair."

"Me, too!"

Kirby was excited to share her invention with her new friends. The bears loved learning to make Flipper Slippers of their own and couldn't wait to try them out. But their laughter woke up Parker.

"What are those things on
your paws?" he growled.

"Flipper Slippers!" said the bears.
"They're toasty warm and tons of fun! Try some!"

Parker shook his head. "Polar Bears have *paws*, not flippers.
I knew something like this would happen.
Start packing, penguin!"

But the polar bears protested. "She can't go now!"

"She's still helping me with my slippers."

"And mine!"

"This could take a while," said Kirby.

"Let her stay!" begged the bears.

"Fine! One penguin. No more!"

Kirby flapped her flippers with glee. She sent a letter to her family telling them about her adventures.

Which is exactly why they came to visit.

Parker was not happy. "Didn't you read the sign?" he asked. "Get out!"

"Wait!" said Kirby. "This is my family."

"We've had a long journey," said the penguins. "Please let us stay."

Parker raised a claw. "One week. No more!" Then he stomped away.

Kirby's family opened their suitcases.
Her friends peeked out of their dens.
"What are you doing?" they asked.

"I'm making my Sled Bed," said Kirby's brother.

"I'm whipping up a batch of snow cones for snack time,"
said Kirby's sister.

"I'm shoveling paths for snow chutes," said Kirby's cousin.

Soon the bears were slurping snow cones, swooshing down snow chutes, and *sleep*-sliding in their Sled Beds. All the bears . . . except for Parker.

"You penguins are taking over this island!" he shouted.
"Pack your bags, hop on your ice floe, and . . .
WHOAAAAAA!"
Parker slipped on some sleet
and crashed to the ice.

"OWWWW!" he cried. "I can't move my leg!"

The polar bears shook their heads. "This never would have happened if you'd been wearing Flipper Slippers."

Kirby and her friends leaped into action. They rolled Parker onto a Sled Bed and shoveled a snow chute to his den.
They pushed his paws into Flipper Slippers and stuffed him with sugary snow cones.

Wow! thought Parker. *This Sled Bed's so snuggly.*
My paws feel so toasty. These snow cones are scrumptious.

In one week, Parker was back on his paws again. The penguins
started packing. They knew their time on Polar Bear Island was up.

"What's going on here?" asked Parker. "Didn't you read the sign?"
The penguins nodded. "Yes. That's why we're leaving."

WELCOME TO
POLAR BEAR ISLAND
~~NO~~ OTHERS ALLOWED

"Maybe you'd better read it again."
Parker pointed to the freshly painted sign.
"I was wrong. You penguins weren't taking over our island.
You were making it a much better place. Please stay."

the CONE cart

So they did.
Penguin & Polar Bear Island became
a wonderful place to live. For **EVERYONE**.